The BLUE Mittens

by Rachel Mann
illustrated by Alexandra Wallner

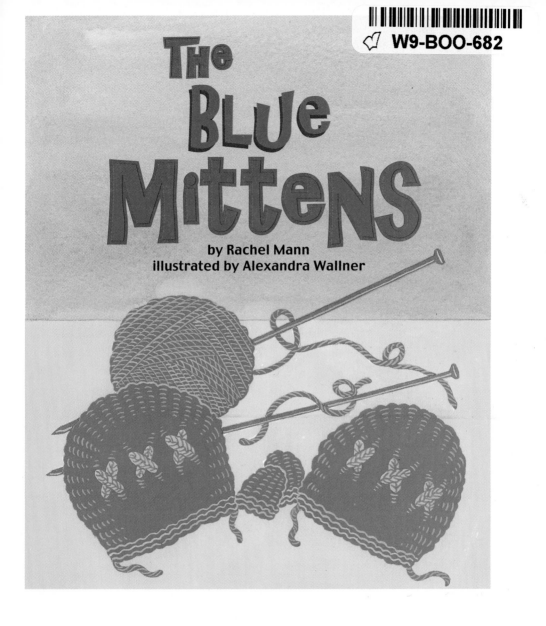

SCHOLASTIC INC.
New York   Toronto   London   Auckland   Sydney
Mexico City   New Delhi   Hong Kong   Buenos Aires

Developed by Kirchoff/Wohlberg, Inc., in cooperation with Scholastic Inc.

Leah jumped out of bed. She ran to see the date.

Yes! It was her birthday. It was her dad's birthday, too. They had the same birthday.

On most days, Leah and her dad did different things. Leah went to school. She liked to jump rope. She liked to put on plays.

Her dad went to work. Her dad liked to fix things. He liked to read the paper.

On their birthday, they did the same thing. They always baked a cake. Leah helped to frost it.

Dad said, "I helped Grandma Rose bake when I was little."

Leah liked to think of her dad as a boy. What was he like? Did he read the paper? Did he fix things?

Dear Grandma Rose,
Today Dad and I baked a cake. It is just like the one he helped you make. It was yummy!
What things did Dad do when he was a boy?
I miss you! Come see us soon!
Love,
Leah

Leah wrote the address on the envelope. She put a stamp on it. Then she mailed it.

Two weeks passed. A letter came in the mail for Leah.

It was from Grandma. Leah was very happy. Grandma wrote stories. Was this another story?

Leah opened the envelope. She saw red paper. Something was wrapped in it.

In the red paper was a pair of mittens.
They were blue. They had white snowflakes
on them. There was a letter, too.

Dear Leah,

I am happy you still make the cake! I remember how Dad loved it. There was one thing he liked more. That was snow. He loved when the snow hid the streets.

He rode his sled. He made snowmen.

I made these mittens for him. He was

eight then. I hope they fit you now.

Have fun in the snow!

Love,
Grandma Rose

Leah put the mittens on. They were her size! They were soft. They had the sweet smell of Grandma Rose.

Leah also loved to play in the snow. She liked thinking of her dad doing that!

"Too bad he's not eight now," she thought to herself.

"What nice mittens!" said Leah's mom.
"How kind of Grandma Rose to make them
for you."

"I think she made those for me!" said
Dad. "Thirty years ago!"

"Do you remember playing in the snow?"
Leah asked him.

"How could I forget?" said her dad.
"There was nothing better than a snowy day."
    Leah looked outside. There was still snow
on the ground.

"Let's make a snowman," Dad said.
"You can put on the blue mittens."
    "What will you put on?" asked Leah.
    Just then the bell rang.

It was Grandma Rose!

"I had a feeling you would need these," she said.

She gave Leah's dad a new pair of mittens. They were just his size.

"Now zip up your coats!" she said.